THE MAKING OF A MISTRESS

LINDA RAE SANDE

The Making of a Mistress

http://www.lindaraesande.com

ISBN: 978-1-946271-47-1

Twisted Teacup Publishing, Cody, Wyoming

Deminon

Diana

CHAPTER 1
AN ASSIGNMENT SURPRISES

March 1815, Whitehall, London

Attempting to soften the sound of her boot heels on the polished stone floor of the wide Home Office corridor, Daisy Albright slowed and regarded the nameplate on the nearest door.

Inhaling, she compared it to the name found at the bottom of the letter she had received only the hour before. Assured it matched, she lifted a gloved fist and knocked.

Not hearing an immediate response, she was about to knock again when she heard, "Come," called out from within. She quietly slipped inside the office, closing the door behind her. As she did in any new environment, she took a moment to look about and study everything she didn't recognize.

Far different from most of the other offices along the

same corridor—this one featured light wood paneling, a Turkish carpet, a massive mahogany desk topped with a large lit lamp near its center, and an upholstered chair where there would usually be a wooden one—Daisy noted the presence of someone at the desk. The lamp prevented her from seeing him completely, but from what she could see, she thought she might have mistaken the name on the letter. About to check the letter again, she froze when she realized she was being watched by said presence.

"Have you an appointment, miss?"

"Only a letter, sir."

The balding man behind the desk half-stood, waving her to the chair opposite his. "Miss Albright, I presume?" he said before reseating himself in what looked like a new leather chair. Daisy was reminded of the squabs in her late mother's town coach.

"I am, Mr. ... Abbot?" she guessed.

"Guilty," he replied. "Glad to know the post is working here in town," he murmured.

At hearing the weariness in his voice, Daisy sensed the civil servant was bored in his position. At least he had to be comfortable in the office, though. She spied a salver with liquor decanters and what appeared to be crystal glasses on a table behind his desk. There was a fireplace, although the lumps of coal currently burning looked as if they wouldn't last past noon.

The most impressive feature in the office was the chandelier. She thought for a moment it had to have come from somewhere else—surely no government offices were regularly equipped with such an elegant fixture.

"Rescued from a chateau in France," Abbot said as he rifled through a stack of papers on his desk. "Before it was burned to the ground."

Daisy arched a brow.

"Ah, here are your orders," he said as he pulled the paper from the stack. He looked up for the first time since she had entered the office and regarded her with a curious expression. "You'll be perfect for this assignment. You'll need to be away from London for a time—"

"That's not a problem."

"Perhaps a year, mayhap more," he went on, ignoring her interruption. "You're going to Yorkshire. Your mark is an aristocrat."

Struggling to maintain an impassive expression, Daisy said, "Very well."

"Ethan Range, Marquess of Plymouth."

She inhaled softly. "What's he done?"

"Seems there's some evidence of smuggled liquor making its way into the country via the coastline of his marquessate," Abbot replied. "We need confirmation before he can be charged. An eye witness who can follow what's happening and report to our agent in Scarborough." He pulled on a pair of spectacles and reviewed another sheet of parchment. "Ah, looks like the Foreign Office has been apprised. With any luck, Chamberlain will have one of his operatives acting on the water. He has an old Navy ship now," he said before he rolled his eyes. "Supposedly auctioned off and dismantled, but it's apparently still in one piece and crewed by pirates." He shook his head. "Why do they get to have all the fun over there?" he murmured rhetorically.

About to counter his words, Daisy elected to remain quiet. She had worked briefly for Chamberlain in the past. After she'd been shot in the leg whilst attempting to deliver orders in Belgium, she'd been left with a slight limp. For that and, well, for another reason entirely unrelated to her qualifications as an operative, Chamberlain had let her go. He had provided a character reference, though, which had her landing a similar position with the Home Office.

"So, your assignment is to get yourself hired as his mistress, stay close, convince him to talk, and catch him in the act."

Daisy nodded. "Very well, sir," she replied.

He passed her an envelope. "No need to change your name for this one unless you want to. There's a ticket for the mail coach. Four days in transit. You'll need to be in Scarborough no later than a week from now. Doesn't give you much time to prepare."

Peering into the envelope, she found several bank notes, some coins, a ticket for the mail coach, and a creme calling card. "The Soho Club, sir?" she asked, pulling the card from the envelope.

"That's where you'll stay until you leave London.

There's a room reserved for you. Three nights. Just ask for Mrs. Skarsgard."

Daisy was about to argue that she had a place to stay—she'd been ensconced in The Coburg since her return to London—but if the Home Office was willing to cover the costs of her accommodations for the next few days, who was she to complain?

"Give you a chance to hone your skills at seduction and... such," Abbot said as he waggled his brows.

At that moment, Daisy remembered the assignment. She cleared her throat. "Has someone been... assigned to... to *be* seduced?"

For the first time since she had entered the office, Abbot grinned. "You'll have see to your own mark for that, Miss Albright," he replied.

"Very good, sir. Is there anything else?"

He shook his head.

Daisy gave him a nod and took her leave of the office, her limp considerably more noticeable now that she had been sitting too long. Once she was in the corridor, she leaned against the wall and took a deep breath.

She was relieved to have an assignment—glad, even—but this one would cost her more than most. Acting as the Marquess of Plymouth's mistress meant she would be sacrificing her virtue.

Father will be furious, she thought.

Well, only if he discovered the truth.

CHAPTER 2
SOHO SO SECRET

An hour later, Soho Square, London

Pulling the creme card from the envelope in her reticule, Daisy read the engraved script of the Soho Club's address and then glanced up at the corresponding building before her. Like White's and the other exclusive clubs in St. James Street, there was no shingle or even a placard to indicate the name of the establishment. The exterior had been recently cleaned, though, the stone free of the past winter's layer of soot.

Making her way to the door, she discovered the card worked rather well. The portly gentleman in front of her was denied entry and waved away from the premises while she received a bow from the footman.

"I'm to ask for Mrs. Skarsgard," she said quietly, once she was inside the wood-paneled vestibule. Although there were hooks on which to hang coats and a bin for umbrellas, there were none there now. There was a desk off to the side, currently unmanned.

"Would you like to leave your redingote, my lady?"

Daisy wondered if the footman used the honorific for all the women who held a creme card or if her accent had given her away. Had she adopted the dialect she had perfected for her assignment in Leeds the year before, he might have merely called her 'miss.' "Thank you, no," she replied.

The doorman opened the next door, revealing what appeared to be an inner sanctum. Sconces lit with candles cast a golden glow along the walls while velvet drapes covered every window. Several chandeliers added their light and warmth, reminding Daisy of a ballroom. An empty one, though, for no one else was there despite an array of upholstered furnishings.

"You can find Mrs. Skarsgard up the stairs and down the hall," the doorman said before he bowed and disappeared through the door from which they had just come.

Daisy was about to ask for better directions, but decided the proprietor's office must be evident. She turned and made her way up the stairs, glad the thick Aubusson carpeting muffled her climb. Back in Whitehall, she had thought everyone along Mr. Abbot's corridor could have heard her approach.

At the top of the stairs, there was only one direction in which to go, and she made her way down the carpeted corridor until she came upon a door with a brass nameplate. She knocked, heartened when a feminine voice said, "Come."

Opening the door, Daisy dared a glance inside before she fully stepped into what could have been a small bedchamber. There was no bed, though. There were two wingback chairs and a small table. A chaise longue sat beneath the room's only window. Although light came through it, the room was mostly lit with candle lamps.

The source of the feminine voice sat at a small escritoire. She stood upon Daisy's arrival, though. "How do?" she said by way of a greeting.

"I'm to ask for Mrs. Skarsgard."

"And found her you have," the woman replied. Set off by a sky blue day gown, black hair, and chocolate brown eyes, Mrs. Skarsgard's caramel skin fairly glowed in the sunlight that streamed through the room's two windows. It also didn't give away her age. She could have been twenty, thirty, or forty years old.

"It's good to make your acquaintance. I am Daisy—"

"We don't use names here," Mrs. Skarsgard interrupted. "Our members are then allowed to be whomever they wish to be without any societal expectations."

"Then how am I to claim the room that has apparently been reserved for me by the Home Office?"

"We've been expecting you," Mrs. Skarsgard stated. She lifted a key from the escritoire and held it out to her. "End of the hall on the right. You have a room with a vantage," she added as Daisy took the proffered key.

"And as I understand the arrangement, you'll be with us for three nights."

Daisy nodded. "Thank you, yes," she replied. "Are there any rules I should know about?"

"No names. No sharing what you might see or hear whilst you're under our roof, and you can be assured of the same consideration from our other club members."

Members.

Daisy wasn't exactly a member, and she was about to say so when Mrs. Skarsgard said, "You are a member during your stay, of course, and welcome to return when you're able. You need only show your card."

Glancing at the creme card she still held clutched in her kid-gloved hand, Daisy furrowed a brow. "What if I require someone to join me on occasion during my stay?"

The older woman shrugged. "You need only give him the card."

Daisy considered that if she gave her card to someone else, she wouldn't be allowed entry, but Mrs. Skarsgard was quick to hold out another creme card. "This card," she clarified.

Daisy took the proffered card, noting it was slightly different from hers. "Very good, ma'am. Thank you." After a pause, she asked, "Could you recommend a place from which I might acquire a breakfast in the mornings?" She already knew of familiar haunts where she was comfortable gaining a late luncheon or a supper, but she was used to breakfast being served in the hotel.

"We're not an uncivilized club, Miss Albright," Mrs. Skarsgard replied brightly. "There's a dining room downstairs, or if you wish, a tray can be delivered to your door."

Not bothering to hide her surprise, Daisy said, "I apologize. I'm not familiar with the arrangements here."

"Of course not, but I do expect you'll find them better than any hotel."

Nodding, Daisy said, "It's a wonder the Home Office can afford such accommodations." Even if their budget was larger than that of the Foreign Office.

"Oh, we are all patriots here, Miss Albright," Mrs. Skarsgard replied. "The Home Office won't be charged for your stay. It's the least we can do for King and Country."

Almost not believing the proprietress, Daisy arched a brow. "How very generous of you," she said. She glanced down at the key and the card she held. "I'll not take any more of your time. Thank you, Mrs. Skarsgard," she added, thinking it rather odd that despite the 'no names' edict, the woman had called her 'Miss Albright' twice, and she hadn't even introduced herself.

Daisy curtsied and took her leave, hurrying down the hall to a room she expected would be no better than a hovel.

Turning the key in the lock, she opened the door and inhaled softly.

For a moment, she wondered if Mrs. Skarsgard knew she would be using this room to prepare for her role as a mistress to a marquess. What else could explain the soft pink silk on the walls? The deep pink velvet counterpane and drapes? The deeper pink curtains around the bed? The gold gilt dressing table and three-paneled japanned screen in the corner?

Daisy almost laughed before she remembered what she would have to do in this room. What she would have to give up.

Not that her virtue was of much value to her.

She had no intention of ever marrying.

Once a suitor discovered who her mother was—or what she had done for a living—he would probably beg off. If he stayed around long enough for her to admit who her father was, then he would either stay because he thought her dowry would have him set for life or because he truly cared for her.

She was too jaded to believe he would stay because he truly cared for her.

No matter her possible future, her current plan required a mark. A man she had to convince to teach her everything she needed to know to be a mistress. A man who valued discretion. A man who would have just as much to lose if her plan didn't work.

Silently blessing Abbot for having mentioned the British ship and pirate crew that would be searching for the smugglers from the water, she knew exactly who she could approach.

He might not be a pirate in his real life, but it was possible she could talk Alexander Bradley, also known as

Captain Jack Crawley, into a few nights of illicit encounters with her.

Deciding she couldn't waste another moment admiring the bedchamber, Daisy took her leave of the Soho Club and made her way back to Whitehall.

CHAPTER 3
LURING A LOVER

An hour later

Daisy stepped from the hackney, careful to lead with her uninjured leg as she allowed the driver to help her down the single step.

She handed him a coin, thankful for the collection of them that had been included in the envelope Mr. Abbot had given her. Although she had some of her own, they were at the bottom of her overstuffed reticule.

"Would you like me to wait for you, my lady?"

Daisy regarded the driver with a look of surprise. She had never known a hackney driver to offer to wait for her. "It's not necessary, sir. I might be an hour or more," she replied. "But thank you for offering."

She wondered about the look of disappointment the driver displayed as he tipped his hat and climbed back on to the bench. Perhaps she had given him a coin of a higher denomination than she had intended. Or mayhap he was merely concerned and thought he should ensure she was safely returned to the Soho Club.

Had she become so hardened in her life as an operative that she couldn't believe the latter? That she believed the former because she usually did see to paying more for a service than was expected? Despite growing up in a life of privilege, she now knew that most people lived lives of poverty.

Turning her gaze onto the small building located in the corner of the Whitehall complex—the Foreign Office was relegated to only a few rooms within—Daisy struggled to tamp down her nervousness before she made her way to the front doors.

ALEXANDER BRADLEY, Foreign Office operative and occasional captain of the pirate ship known as the *Molly*, regarded the stack of paperwork on his desk and audibly sighed.

"The longer you ignore it, the higher it will rise," Matthew Fitzsimmons, Viscount Chamberlain, warned when he passed Alex's desk.

Despite the chiding rebuke, Alex gave his boss—and the head of the Foreign Office—a nod of acknowledgement. "Yes, my lord."

Chamberlain paused in his pursuit of his office and returned to stand before Alex. "We've just received word from Home that they have their operative set to depart for Scarborough in a few days."

Alex stood and gave the viscount a bow. "A few days, sir?"

"Time to muster your crew, Bradley."

Alex resisted the urge to roll his eyes. "The *Molly* has been in the docks in Wapping since last week, sir. A couple of repairs to her hull and a new sail, and she'll be ready for her next assignment."

"Good, because I'm about to sign the orders for you to leave our company." He indicated the stack of papers. "But not until your paperwork is complete."

Hissing, and not apologizing for it, Alex gave the viscount a quelling glance. "You do know it's not as fun as you're making it out to be."

Lord Chamberlain let out a loud guffaw. "So says the man who can't wait to be aboard the *Molly*."

The viscount had him there. Months of desk duty had Alex chomping at the bit to return to the water. To engage in pursuing pirates and smugglers, kidnappers and rogues, in the hopes of acquiring their bounty and arresting the ruffians. It didn't matter that for every ship he and his crew disabled or secured for the British Foreign Office, three or four others went undeterred in their missions to shortchange the British government.

"You know me too well, sir," Alex replied as he took his seat.

He watched the viscount make his way to his modest

office, deciding he really couldn't curse the man. He was only doing his job.

Returning to his own, Alex was about to pluck the next paper from the stack when a hint of feminine perfume wafted past his nostrils. He glanced up, wondering how he had missed the arrival of the young woman who stood on the other side of his desk.

"Miss Albright?" he asked in surprise. He quickly stood even as she waved him down.

"Really, Mr. Bradley. You needn't stand on my account," Daisy murmured. She eyed a nearby chair and was about to pull it toward the desk, but Alex beat her to it.

"I must, and I will," he said as he held the chair for her. "It's been an age since I've seen you," he added as Daisy took the proffered chair.

Alex regarded the Home Office operative with an assessing glance, heartened to see the job hadn't aged her prematurely. No more than five-foot-one in her heeled slippers, the dark-haired English miss might have been twenty or thirty years in age. He was fairly sure she was halfway in between.

"And yet you appear exactly as I remember you," she countered playfully.

"Ah, a woman after my heart. Or something else?" he said with suspicion in his voice.

Daisy regarded the stack of papers on his desk. "You really need to hire a secretary, Mr. Bradley."

"If Chamberlain actually paid me, I might hire one," he countered with a smirk.

The words had Daisy considering how she might secure his services. "Have you received any orders yet?"

He narrowed his eyes. "I've been warned I will, but my lack of a secretary prevents me from being bestowed with them." A hand waved over the papers. "Apparently I must clear my desk before Chamberlain will allow me to resume my position as captain of the *Molly*."

"For a mission off the coast of Yorkshire, mayhap?" she asked in a whisper.

Alex stilled himself. His gaze darting around them, he finally leaned forward and said, "What do you know of it?"

"I received my orders from Abbot earlier today. I'm to depart for Scarborough in a few days. Felix Snelling will be my contact there."

"For?"

She gave him a quelling glance. "A mission, of course."

"Who is your mark?"

Inhaling slowly, Daisy whispered, "Plymouth—"

"The marquess?"

"Indeed," she confirmed. "They suspect he's running a smuggling operation."

"That's ridiculous," Alex said, scoffing. "The man owns coal mines. Huge properties. He has no need of funds from illegal liquor."

"Agreed," Daisy replied, rather surprised he mentioned liquor. She hadn't when she had broached the subject, which meant he had already been told the particulars of his upcoming mission. "Nevertheless, I'm to get as close to him as possible. Ensure I am hired as his mistress."

For the briefest of moments, Daisy was sure she saw anger—or was that jealousy?—in the other operative's eyes. "Discover what I can and report to an agent in Scarborough. Abbot says I can expect it might take as long as a year."

Alex stared at her for several seconds before he said, "Now I know why I'm being dispatched seaside." At her questioning glance, he added, "I might be a master of disguises, but I rather doubt the man would take *me* on as his mistress."

Daisy rolled her eyes. She had never seen him in a gown and wig, but given Alex's skills, he probably could pass himself off as a woman—at least until it came time to disrobe. "You underestimate yourself, Mr. Bradley," she chided.

When Daisy didn't say anything more, Alex leaned over his desk. "So why are you here?"

Inhaling, she pulled out the creme card Mrs. Skarsgard had given to her at the Soho Club. "I need your help," she said. She handed the card to him. "And apparently you need mine," she added as she pointed to the stack of papers.

Alex stared at the card, his dark brows furrowing. "The Soho Club," he murmured.

"Have you been there?"

He shrugged. "Once. A long time ago."

Daisy dipped her head. "I have a room there. For the next few days."

"I didn't realize they offered overnight accommodations," Alex whispered.

The words sent a pleasant shiver down Daisy's spine. "My room is decorated in shades of pink and features a good deal of gold gilt," she said, arching a brow in an initial attempt at seduction.

"Sounds like it could be a young miss' bedchamber. Or a brothel," he remarked.

"Oh, good. Because for the next few nights, it needs to be the latter," Daisy replied with a smirk.

CHAPTER 4
REELING HIM IN

A moment later

Alex stared at Daisy. "Come again?"

"I would, but it seems I haven't yet *cum* for the first time," she replied, her smirk still apparent.

His brows furrowing, Alex shook his head. "What's this about?"

"I need you. Or... your skills. In bed."

A grin replaced his look of curiosity. "I wasn't aware my reputation preceded me," he teased.

"You're a man, Mr. Bradley. One who has been blessed by handsome good looks and a pleasant manner. The dental gods obviously love you—"

"Oh, you wouldn't say that if you had seen me when Jack Crawley is wearing his gold teeth," he said with a tentative grin, his manner no longer so jovial. "I rather doubt those gods would approve of my appearance then."

"And I believe you have experience which can only benefit me for this assignment," Daisy went on, ignoring his comment about the gold teeth. She had seen him once in his guise as Crawley and thought the gold more comical than intimidating, but then she knew what lay under those dentures.

Alex blinked. "Something tells me you're not referring to my experience as a pirate." When her brows arched as if she was about to claim it did, the operative leaned forward and lowered his voice to a whisper. "What's this about?"

Once again, Daisy surveyed their surroundings. "I am in need of someone to instruct me."

"To do what?"

"Seduce a man. Convince him I would be the perfect mistress. And then proceed to actually perform as a mistress. Believably."

Alex stared at her for a long moment. "I rather imagine you already possess the seduction skills, Miss Albright."

"If I do, I'm not aware of them," she replied.

"Trust me. You don't need to be," he claimed. "The way you walk? With that slight limp? The way your hips sway does all the talking for you." He pantomimed with his hands what he meant.

Daisy's eyes widened in shock.

"Oh, don't look so surprised, Miss Albright," he

chided. "There's always a trail of drool that must be mopped up from behind you," he teased.

She almost turned to look behind her, but managed to resist the urge when she noticed the twinkle in his eye. "I hadn't noticed."

He rolled his eyes in mock disbelief. "The pretty ones never do," he murmured.

Daisy couldn't decide if his comment was meant as a compliment or a cut. The word 'pretty' could be used for either. The fact that she couldn't completely read him had her even more intrigued with him. "Will you assist me when it comes to what happens in a bed, Mr. Bradley?"

His eyes stopped rolling and immediately rounded. "*What*?"

"I need to learn," she said. "How to... to be a mistress. What's expected of me." She might have learned everything she needed to know from her mother had the former courtesan lived long enough.

And if her father had been someone other than who he was.

If he had any idea what she was proposing, she was sure he would have her locked up in a cottage in Kent with two large guards. Her only means of escape would have been by marriage.

Managing to hide his immediate discomfort at the topic of their conversation, Alex shrugged. "Well, you just have to... to make love to him," he said, wincing when he remembered who her mark was. Ethan Range,

Marquess of Plymouth.

The marquess wasn't a bad sort. He wasn't an old curmudgeon or a scoundrel. He was on the younger side —probably less than five-and-thirty—but he was married to his marquessate. The lack of gossip surrounding him suggested he lived a quiet life on the moors. His drafty domicile, known as Castle Keyes, had existed since Henry the VIII's reign.

If Plymouth had done anything of note, Alex wasn't aware of it. The man hadn't even claimed his seat in Parliament, apparently so overwhelmed with looking after a marquessate that had been poorly managed by his father that he had no time to make trouble.

"Your assessment of my skills is to be questioned, Mr. Bradley, especially since we've never had the opportunity to engage in such activities," Daisy argued.

"Not because I didn't wish to," he murmured.

Daisy's eyes widened slightly. "So... you wish to? Share a bed with me?"

He cleared his throat. "There isn't a red-blooded man in London who would deny you," he claimed.

"Oh, this is such a relief," she said on a sigh, sitting back in her chair. "I feared you would dismiss me outright," she added.

"Why?"

She allowed a slight shrug. "What could possibly be in it for you but a tumble, I suppose?"

Alex's gaze darted to the stack of papers. Before he could say anything, Daisy added, "And the opportunity for your own private secretary to see to your paper-work?" As bribes went, it wasn't the best, but at the moment, it was the only one she could devise.

"You say that as if you already know you're cleared to see some of this rot," he accused.

"I probably am."

Allowing a slight grin, Alex asked, "When do we start?"

"Can you come to the Soho Club tonight?" She pointed to the creme card she had given him. "Just show it to the doorman, and he'll admit you. I'm upstairs. Take a right at the top of the stairs. My room is at the end of the hall on the right."

Furrowing a brow, Alistair said, "I've an appointment at Brooks's, but I won't be long there."

"Good, because I still have to move my things from The Coburg. I'm going there next."

"Careful, Miss Albright. You might have become a creature of habit."

She winced. "I haven't stayed at The Coburg in an age. No one who works there now was there when I was last in residence," she argued. "And besides, it was Gril-lion's back then."

Not about to argue—he knew he would lose against a former colleague—Alex glanced at his pocket watch. "Nine o'clock?"

"I'll be ready," she replied. Then her eyes rounded. "What should I wear?"

Alex scoffed. "If I answer that, you'll slap my face," he

said in a hoarse whisper, one of his dark brows arching. "Hard."

The oddest sensation darted down Daisy's spine just then, and she inhaled softly. "Nine o'clock it is. Don't forget the paperwork."

Without another word, and before Alex could stand from his chair, Daisy was up and out of hers, making her way to the nearest exit as she struggled to keep from limping.

She wasn't about to afford Mr. Bradley a view of swaying hips as she took her leave.

CHAPTER 5
SHOPPING FOR A SEDUCTION

Outside of Whitehall

At the curb, Daisy was stunned to discover the hackney in which she had ridden to Whitehall was parked near the corner.

Suspicious, Daisy made her way to the driver and angled her head, about to chide him for waiting. But when he moved to open the door, a passenger stepped out and paid him before hurrying off.

"Where to, miss?" the driver asked.

"The Coburg," she replied. "Go by way of New Bond Street, won't you? I need to make a quick purchase at one of the ladies' shops."

The driver arched a brow. "Ah, mayhap the one with the, uh, *underthings*?" he asked, his face visibly reddening.

Daisy allowed a slow smile to appear, wondering if

what she was doing could be considered seduction. "Why, I suppose that's the place."

Not having been anywhere near New Bond Street in over a year, she had no idea what shops might feature ladies undergarments these days, but she thought it was the best place to start. She needed to find something she could wear later that evening. Her virginal white nigh-trail would not suit when it came to seducing Alexander Bradley.

Try as she might, Daisy hadn't been able to discern exactly what Alex implied with his comment, *If I answer that, you'll slap my face.*

Had he intended to say something scandalous, like 'nothing at all' or 'bed linens'? She didn't know if she dared answer the door naked, but she thought back to how she remembered her mother garbed for the nights she was expecting to entertain Daisy's father.

The gowns Lily Albright had worn were definitely French. Diaphanous. Nearly as sheer as a silk chemise but floor-length. Cut low in the neck and lower at the back. One was edged with fluffy feathers, and the slippers she had worn featured the same balls of fluff atop her toes.

Daisy thought of how much blunt she had in her reticule. Surely she would have enough to purchase such a gown.

Despite the heavy afternoon traffic, the hackney driver seemed determined to get her to the shop in record time. Did he think she was going to model her acquisition for him?

Before she could even finish the thought, the hackney pulled up in front of a shop which displayed stays and a petticoat in its window. The equipage stuttered to a halt.

"You will wait for me?" she asked when the driver opened the door.

"Oh, yes, my lady."

Struck by how he addressed her, Daisy wondered if he had mistaken her for someone else. She did look a great deal like her youngest aunt, Elise, but the woman had several years on her. "I shouldn't be long."

Acting as if he didn't care if she spent the night in the shop, the driver made his way to the front of the horses and gave each a small apple.

Glad he saw to his matched pair—most hackney drivers didn't even water their horses during the course of their day—Daisy entered the shop of underthings and immediately paused inside the door.

If she had thought her room at the Soho Club was pink, she now knew it couldn't possibly hold a candle to the pink boudoir that was spread out before her. Barely taking another step inside—enough so she wouldn't block the door—she allowed her gaze to sweep the shop. Spotting the area where gowns for bedchambers were hung on a series of pegs, she was about to make her way toward them when the proprietress intersected her path.

"May I be of assistance?"

Deciding she could afford a moment's delay, Daisy said, "Why, yes. I'm in need of a translucent gown suitable for a seduction."

Expecting the woman to react in horror, she was stunned when the shopkeeper said, "This way." After a few steps, she turned and asked, "Have you a color in mind? I have quite a selection."

A memory of one of her mother's French gowns came to mind. It had been a light shade of blue. She was about to mention it when the shopkeeper lowered her voice to a whisper and said, "White is always very popular, followed by red."

Daisy's eyes widened. "White?" she repeated.

"Even when men know they're not about to bed a virgin, they can still pretend."

Of course some men preferred a virgin every time they tupped a woman, but Daisy was fairly sure Alex Bradley wasn't one of them. "And if they are?" she countered. "Still a virgin," she added when the shopkeeper gave her an odd glance.

The woman looked confused for a moment, as if she had never hosted a virgin in the shop. "Why, pale blue, I suppose," she murmured. She waved toward a painted shelf on which a few muslin gowns were folded so their bodices were apparent. None of them looked particularly scandalous.

Daisy's attention went to a sheer confection. She was sure it was the same color as her mother's, and she thought to buy it before she realized she would think of her mother every time she wore it.

Spotting a gown in red satin, she inhaled sharply.

"It has a matching dressing gown, although the wrapper is sheer," she shopkeeper said. "As are for all of these French negligées." She shook out the gown and held it in front of Daisy. "Or you could simply wear the wrapper, I suppose," she added, opening it to reveal a red feather edging.

Sure she was blushing the same color as the sheer dressing gown, Daisy said, "I'd like to buy that, please." She almost asked about slippers to wear with it, but thought better of it. Surely she would have time to shop for those in Scarborough.

"Very well," the shopkeeper said as she led Daisy to the front counter. Daisy watched as the woman wrote out a receipt. The blunt in the envelope was more than enough to cover the cost, which had Daisy second-guessing her choice.

"I'd like a white one as well. With a robe. And the purple and the royal blue."

The shopkeeper's eyes rounded. "Of course. Would you like anything else?"

"White silk stockings with the ribbons at the top."

The woman paused in her writing, one of her blonde brows arching in approval. "I'll get those for you right away." She left the counter to retrieve the garments while Daisy dared a look out the window. As promised, the hackney was still parked out front, the driver checking the harnesses and leads as the horses stomped their impatience.

A few minutes later, she left the shop with a flat pasteboard box, her purchases folded and encased in a length of tissue paper inside.

ONCE SHE WAS in the hotel room at The Coburg, she fished some coins from the bottom of her reticule and slipped them into her glove. Gathering her limited array of toiletries and the clothes she had unpacked the day before, she took one last look around before departing the hotel.

Back out in front of The Coburg, she was stunned to discover the hackney still parked there. She had already paid the driver, expecting he would wish to take on more fares that afternoon. "You didn't need to wait for me," Daisy said, hoping she didn't sound as if she were scolding the man.

"Actually, I did, my lady. Strict instructions from Mrs. Skarsgard."

The driver moved to take her valise from her while Daisy stared at him. His words had been so unexpected, she didn't have a chance to feign indifference. "Are you employed by the Soho Club?" she asked. She supposed it shouldn't be a surprise that the club would have its own means of transportation. Some of the better shops in

London offered carriages for their clients' use on occasion.

"You could say that, my lady," he replied as he placed her bag inside the coach and did the same with the pasteboard box. He offered his hand. "Wouldn't want you fleeced by an unscrupulous driver."

Daisy accepted his help—her leg was sore, and she didn't trust it for the climb into the coach. "Much appreciated, sir."

"Do you wish to dine now, my lady?"

Not having given a thought to an evening meal, Daisy was about to shake her head and then remembered she would be entertaining in her room later that evening. "Where might I find champagne?"

As if the driver expected such a query, he replied, "I would suggest Berry Brothers in Jermyn Street, my lady, but I have it on good authority there are several bottles set aside for your consumption at the club."

Daisy's eyes rounded. "But..." She was about to argue that she rarely drank the stuff, but thought better of it. Someone obviously thought she was there to live the high life. Hard to believe the Home Office could afford such an extravagance, though.

So... if not her employer, then who?

The driver's eyes darted sideways before he leaned into the coach and said, "*All* of the rooms at the club include a selection of liquors, my lady."

Emitting a sigh of relief, Daisy afforded him an appreciative glance. "How civilized," she murmured. "I think I would like to go back to the club now." With several hours until her appointment with Mr. Bradley, she could take the time to properly bathe and dress her hair. Mayhap partake of a glass or two of champagne whilst she waited.

She watched as the driver bowed and closed the door, curious if he thought this was her first time in London. Perhaps her behavior on this day was that of a new arrival to the capital—wide-eyed and innocent.

If only he knew, she thought as she settled into the squabs for the short trip to Soho Square.

CHAPTER 6
AN OPERATIVE
PREVARICATES

Meanwhile, back at the Foreign Office

Cursing softly when Daisy managed to take her leave without displaying so much as single sway of her hips, Alex sat back in his chair and inter-laced his fingers.

He glanced down at what they surreptitiously covered. His arousal had begun the moment Daisy had appeared in front of his desk. He couldn't even fathom why the woman had such an effect on him. She was pretty, but not beautiful like the typical blonde misses who made up most of the daughters of the *ton*. Her dark hair may have had something to do with it, but he couldn't imagine her as a blonde. She had probably played one on occasion—she was known at the office for her varied disguises, many dependent on the high-quality wigs she managed to acquire.

Which had him briefly wondering how she could afford them. Pay was shite for the kind of work they did, which meant most of the operatives had some other source of income. An inheritance or a patron who saw to their expenses.

For some reason he hadn't before considered, Alex had always thought Daisy was a former guttersnipe, an orphan who someone had plucked from the streets and taught to be a keen observer.

When he had first met her, she had been on the lean side, as if she had never been fed her fill. After another assignment, he noted how she had filled out in all the right places. Then, after what had happened in Belgium —after Wellington's battle against Napoleon's forces— Daisy had begun displaying the slight limp that had him forgetting whatever it was he was supposed to be remembering.

A quick review of that mission had him learning she'd been shot in the leg—by a traitor. One of four agents who had been dispatched with the same message for Wellington at the front lines, Daisy hadn't made it with hers.

Although she had recovered from her wound and seemed eager to resume her work, the distinctive limp sometimes gave her away. Made her a liability for most missions.

Made her perfect for this one.

For a moment, Alex rather wished *he* was the Marquess of Plymouth.

No other woman had ever had him so curious. So damned aroused.

He wondered at her appearance again.

Perhaps he wasn't attracted to the typical English miss. Perhaps his attentions should go to dark-haired young women with alluring eyes and hips that swayed with every step.

He groaned and then turned his attention to the stacks of papers on his desk—letters and reports, forms and briefs. Daisy had said to bring them. She had been serious with her offer to see to them, and he knew she could. Knew she could be trusted with whatever intelligence they contained.

But before he left for his appointment, he thought to at least review what he was going to leave in her care. Leave for her to complete, to write letters or whatever needed to be done. He didn't dare pass off what Lord Chamberlain expected *him* to finish.

Another thought struck him, which had him pulling a small sheet of paper from a desk drawer. With a dip of his pen, he wrote a quick note and set it aside, chuckling as he did so.

He pulled several sheets of Foreign Office parchment from his desk along with a quill and an ink pot, knowing he would need to supply Daisy with the tools to do the job.

Although he supposed the Soho Club was probably equipped with some of the more civilized accoutrements, he wasn't about to assume anything. If they did have their own stationery for their guests' use, he didn't want his letters to be written on it. He wouldn't be able to maintain his carefully crafted guise of a man barely able to pay his bills.

The thought of disguises had him considering if he knew anything more about Daisy Albright. If she had been an orphan as he suspected, then there would be no family ties. Nothing to keep her from taking on missions those with families could not.

But what if she wasn't? What if there were parents? Siblings? Children?

The last thought had scoffing.

"Was that Miss Albright I just saw taking her leave?"

Alex nearly jumped from his chair, which actually helped him rise at the sudden appearance of Matthew Fitzsimmons, Viscount Chamberlain. "Indeed, sir," he replied. "She was apprising me of her next assignment. One that dovetails nicely with mine, as it happens."

The oddest expression crossed the viscount's face before he cleared his throat. "Plymouth?" he guessed.

Alex nodded. "Home has her assigned to Scarborough to... watch him. For as long as a year, apparently." He deliberately didn't mention her real mission—to get herself hired as Plymouth's mistress—thinking Chamberlain's reaction rather odd.

Chamberlain hissed. "If that's all, then good," he murmured.

"Sir?"

His eyes darting to the stack of papers on the desk,

the viscount said, "Best you clear your desk, Bradley. You don't want to leave her up there all alone."

Alex furrowed a brow. "She won't be, sir. She'll be reporting to Snelling."

The viscount pretended indifference. "You're still reporting to *me*," Chamberlain stated, his head jerking to indicate the papers.

"I'm on it, sir." He wondered about the viscount's lack of reaction to hearing that Home's operative, Felix Snelling, would be Daisy's contact in Scarborough. Although he didn't know the man well, he knew Snelling would step in and rescue Daisy should it become necessary.

While Viscount Chamberlain made his way back to his office, Alex quickly rifled through the papers, setting aside those he could trust Daisy to manage and keeping those he knew he would need to see to personally.

An hour later, he inserted his hastily written note in between sheets towards the bottom of Daisy's share—nearly three-quarters of the stack—and stuffed them into a satchel before taking his leave of the office.

Although he had two appointments to attend to this evening and could show up for both in the same clothes he was currently wearing, he had decided something more decorative—more formal—was called for when it came to the second appointment.

"Arthur's," he called out when a hackney pulled up to the curb in front of Whitehall.

"Very good, sir," the driver replied.

ALTHOUGH ARTHUR'S wasn't as posh as White's or as elegant as Brooks's, it was a men's club. And it featured accommodations appropriate for a bachelor who couldn't afford the more expensive rooms at The Albany or the more restrictive rules at a boarding house run by a widow.

"Would you like me to wait, sir?" the driver asked after he opened the door to the hackney.

Taken aback by the unusual offer, Alex stared at the middle-aged man. "That won't be necessary." After a pause, he added, "But I will be going out again in about an hour," he said. "If you're here..."

"Very good, sir," the driver replied, tipping his hat when his fare paid him a bit more than was expected.

Alex made his way into the club and to the staircase at the back. He quickly negotiated the two flights that led to his rooms and winced when he noted the clock on the mantel. He didn't have time for the full shower bath he usually enjoyed a few mornings every week, but he could wash most of his body and reapply his cologne.

If it had been one of the summer months, he would have opted for Limes, a scent he had procured from Floris. But given the chill in the air and the likelihood he wouldn't be subjected to an overheated argument during his first appointment, he opted for the spicier Bay Rum scent.

Changing into his Nankeen breeches, a waistcoat

suitable for a *ton* ball, and a topcoat of navy blue superfine, Alex regarded his reflection in the small shaving mirror in his bathing chamber and hoped his appearance wouldn't be misinterpreted by his first appointment.

His attentions to his clothing had everything to do with his second appointment—he didn't want to leave her with a poor impression.

Alex found a short top hat and helped himself to his only cane. The carved walking stick doubled as a weapon when necessary—a knife was concealed beneath one end—although he doubted he would have to use it on this night. His leather satchel would make for an awkward addition when he met with his first appointment, but it couldn't be helped. There were too many papers to stuff into his waistcoat pockets.

Remembering he needed the creme card for entry into the Soho Club, he fished it from his other waistcoat's pocket along with his watch and purse.

Darkness had engulfed the city by the time he made it out of Arthur's, but the lantern hanging on the side of a hackney had him hurrying up to discover it was the same in which he had ridden earlier that evening. "Good timing," he said to the familiar driver.

"Where to, sir?"

"Brooks's." If he'd had more time, he could have walked. The two clubs weren't that far from one another.

～

Five minutes later

ALTHOUGH HE WASN'T a member of the Whig's bastion, Alex gained entry into Brooks's with a mere mention of whom he was to meet. A footman motioned to where his appointment was ensconced in a wingback chair and took his drink order.

"Ah, right on time," Alonyius Abbot said as Alex approached. The Home Office handler already held a drink, and tendrils of smoke floated from a cheroot on an ashtray stand set next to him. "I feared my note might not have reached you this morning."

"Good to see you, sir," Alex replied as he held out his hand. "Your missive not only reached me, but so did its subject earlier this afternoon."

Abbot furrowed a dark brow as he shook Alex's hand. "I'm not sure I'm glad to hear that," he replied.

"Be glad. Miss Albright is all about duty, and she's no fool. She was quick to surmise just who was going to be patrolling the waters during her mission and wished to meet with me."

"Does that often happen?" Abbot asked. He inhaled smoke from the cheroot and blew it out off to the side.

"I haven't seen Miss Albright since before her last assignment with us," Alex claimed, hoping the man couldn't see through his white lie. "Before Belgium."

"Well, I wanted to let you know that she accepted the assignment, but I suppose you already know that." Abbot paused while a footman handed Alex his drink.

Once the servant left their area, he added, "Will you be seeing her again?"

Keeping his expression as impassive as possible, Alex allowed a slight shrug. "Should I, sir?"

Abbot rolled his eyes. "She has to be believable in the role, which means I expect she's off seducing someone as we speak. Thought maybe she'd go to you."

About to clear his throat, Alex instead took a long sip from his drink. "She's very adept at disguises. I rather doubt any man she tempts with her wiles will even recognize her if he saw her again."

"If you say so," Abbot replied on a sigh.

Alex leaned forward and placed his elbows on his knees. "Are you worried she'll fail in the field? Because she won't," he said in a low voice.

"She did in Belgium."

Jerking his head back as if the man had slapped him, Alex scoffed. "Because she was shot in the leg," he countered, rather glad he didn't work for Home.

This bit of news seemed to surprise Abbot, though, as he straightened in his chair. "Shot?"

"In the leg, which is why... why she has such an intriguing way of walking," Alex explained, one of his brows arching suggestively.

"Oh," Abbot replied, his attention going to his empty glass. "I don't believe *that* bit of information was included in the file that was sent over." He noted Alex's glass was empty. "Would you like another?"

Alex shook his head. "I've another appointment this evening. Was there anything else, sir?"

Abbot regarded Alex for a moment before he responded. "When you're done galavanting about playing pirates, do consider stepping up to an office position," he encouraged. "The pay is so much better, and we could always use a good judge of character in our ranks."

Surprised by the offer, Alex dipped his head. "Thank you, sir. I'll keep that in mind."

Alex took his leave of Brooks's, now *very* glad he didn't work for the Home Office. He had no desire to give up playing a pirate, especially in favor of piloting a desk.

CHAPTER 7
AWKWARD BUT NOT AWFUL

Nine o'clock on the dot, Soho Club

Daisy regarded her reflection in the cheval mirror and gave a start. Instead of wearing a blonde wig—she had a thought Mr. Bradley was attracted to blondes—she had opted to simply dress her own dark locks so that only the top half of her hair was arranged in a messy bun. The rest hung in waves past her shoulders.

The red satin gown fit, although it was a bit snug in the low-cut neckline. The rest of it flowed to the floor, hiding her slipper-clad feet. Translucent but for the lace detailing at the edge of the sleeves and down the front opening, the red dressing gown was a perfect match. That some women opted to wear only it to greet their paramours had Daisy wondering if she should have done the same for this night.

The thought of Alex seeing her in such a costume had her nipples hardening into pebbles, and a slight throb developed where her thighs met. Inhaling softly at the reminder of what he would be doing to her that night had the throb increasing in intensity. Her skin flushing with excitement. One hand moving to cover a breast whose nipple was clearly silhouetted in the red satin.

Pound-pound-pound.

The sensation in her ears brought back memories of the assignments she'd been on in the past. The times where danger had her adrenaline rushing and her heart pounding. The rush she had felt had been intoxicating. Addictive. Which is why she supposed she still wanted to take on assignments for the Home Office. No other life, especially the one her father would have preferred she live, would offer the same excitement.

Something caught her attention, and her gaze went to the door. The pounding she had thought was her pulse in her ears wasn't, but rather a knuckle knocking on the door.

Giving her reflection another quick glance, she winced at seeing her arousal was still evident. Well, it couldn't be helped. She took the five steps to the door and opened it a few inches, enough to confirm Alexander Bradley stood on the other side of it.

"I come bearing gifts," he said as Daisy opened the door wider. His expression immediately changed to one of awe as his gaze went from her face to the hem of her gown and back up again. He visibly swallowed, and Daisy was sure she heard the sound of a gulp.

Apparently, the choice of a red gown was the right one.

"Then do come in," Daisy replied. She dipped a curtsy, her quick glance at what he held in one hand barely registering as she regarded him with appreciation. He held a cane and a satchel in the other while a top hat was tucked beneath one arm.

She had expected he would be wearing the same clothes as he had been wearing at the office, but he had changed into more formal attire. Then she recalled his mention of having another appointment before this one.

Whoever he had seen must have been someone important.

Alex blinked and seemed about to say something, but when nothing came out, Daisy took hold of his arm and pulled him into the room. "Are those for me?"

The query seemed to have the desired effect, for Alex gave a start and turned to stare at the hot house daisies he held in one gloved hand. "They are," he replied before holding them out to her.

Daisy nearly giggled, her nervousness settling into something more manageable. "How thoughtful. And original," she teased as she accepted the bouquet of daisies. Given not a single bloom was wilted, she knew Alex hadn't purchased them from a flower girl on the street but rather from a florist. "Would you like some champagne? Or... or a brandy, perhaps?"

The suggestion of liquor seemed to bring him out of his stupor. "Champagne?" he repeated. He belatedly bowed and took her free hand to his lips before glancing around the pink room. Spotting the liquor bottles and a bucket containing the champagne, he moved in that direction. "I would. I haven't been to a ball in an age," he added as he pulled the bottle from its cold bath. "Ice, even?" he asked, turning to stare at her again.

Daisy allowed a shrug, hoping the flowers hid her overt arousal. "I'll put these into a vase," she said as she moved to one of the two dressers on the long wall of the room. She threaded the stems into a ceramic vase that looked as if Wedgwood himself had created it. Free of the flowers, she took her time pouring water into the vase from the dressing table pitcher. She was about to arrange the blooms, but a cold glass pressed against the back of her hand and she nearly gasped.

How had she not heard her guest approach?

"Thank you," she murmured as she took the champagne from him. She touched her glass to the rim of his.

"What are we drinking to?" Alex asked. At some point, he had set aside his hat, cane, and satchel and had removed his gloves.

"Seduction?" she suggested.

He quirked a brow. "Seduction," he agreed. He took a sip of the champagne and then a longer one, nearly downing all the liquor from his glass. "That gown," he said as a finger reached out to touch the translucent muslin of the robe, "does the job, Daisy."

"Oh, what a relief," she replied.

He gave her a quelling glance. "Surely, you knew," he accused.

Daisy took another sip of the champagne. "I wasn't sure. I bought a white one, as well," she replied. "A few others. The shopkeeper said there are men who would find white appealing."

"White?" he repeated, his face displaying a look of confusion.

"I was told it suggested virtue," she replied, arching a dark brow.

Alex considered the comment a moment. "I suppose. If a man wasn't as jaded as I have apparently become."

Daisy sobered, surprised by his words. "Jaded? You're hardly old enough," she said in a quiet voice.

He allowed a shrug before he finished off the champagne. "Now I've gone and made myself sound like a curmudgeon," he murmured.

"Would you like more?"

Alex stared at his glass. "Are you nervous?"

"Of course," she replied. "I've never done anything like this."

One brow furrowing, Alex said, "Neither have I." When he caught her look of surprise, he added, "You may think me a man of the world, and I am to some extent, but I rarely engage in these sorts of *affaires*. And never with anyone I know."

Daisy imagined all the ports of call the *Molly* visited when Captain Jack Crawley was at the helm. Probably every seaside city on the Mediterranean, France, and England. Did he have a favorite woman at every one? Or did he...?

"I do not have a woman in every port of call," he said as he refilled his champagne and then brought the bottle to refill hers.

Visibly reddening, as if she was sure he had read her mind, Daisy said, "But you must have a favorite?"

He screwed up his face a moment. "I rather doubt any of them are still where I last left them," he countered. At her look of disbelief, he added, "I did have a favorite in Spain. She's married now, though, and has four children, last I heard."

"Oh, dear," Daisy murmured, shocked to discover she had already drained the glass he had just poured. He raised the bottle and filled the glass again.

"Careful, Miss Albright. I shouldn't want to be accused of taking advantage," he said as he set the bottle back in the bucket.

"Call me Daisy, please."

Alex regarded her a moment. "Call me Alex."

"And when we're in bed?" she countered, her eyes darkening.

He moved back to stand before her. "Alex. Or... darling," he said with a smirk. "As long as you don't call me by a curse word."

Daisy gave him a brilliant grin. She set down her glass and moved to stand before him. Reaching out, she undid the buttons of his top coat. "If I do anything wrong, you will let me know?" She easily untied the mail coach knot of his cravat.

"I rather doubt you could do anything wrong, Daisy," he whispered as he divested himself of the top coat. He watched as she undid each button of his waistcoat, well aware that his cock knew exactly what she was doing. When she had the last button undone, he pulled the garment from his shoulders and tossed it to a nearby chair. "Most men are just glad to know there will be a woman to warm their bed," he added as he watched the silk cravat unwind from around his neck.

If she hadn't done this before, she had certainly seen a cravat put into place by a valet. Given she was so much shorter than he was, she had to stand on tiptoe to pull the silk from around the back of his neck, and every time she did, the front of her body brushed against his. Despite the fabric of his shirt and the satin of her gown separating them, the feeling of her warmth against his chest sent shivers of desire coursing beneath his skin. "You're killing me," he whispered. Then a groan erupted from his throat, and the fingers of one hand pushed through his dark hair. "I've just realized I've..." He sighed.

"What is it?"

He sighed again. "I meant to bring a French letter," he whispered. "But I promise you, I don't have any awful diseases—"

"Neither do I," Daisy interrupted, heartened he had at least thought about protecting her. Who knew what he might have picked up from one of those ports of call?

"We haven't talked about what would happen should I get a child on you," he murmured.

"My courses just finished yesterday," she replied, her regard for him rising another fraction. If she wasn't careful, she would find herself in love with the honorable man. "You needn't worry about fathering a bastard," she teased.

Alex stayed her hands, preventing them from moving to the fastenings of his breeches. "Have a care, Daisy. I would take you to wife before a babe is born."

Daisy's eyes rounded. "You would?" She didn't mean for the query to make it sound as if she didn't believe him, but she couldn't help it.

His brows furrowed. "I am sorry you seem so surprised." The sound of his disappointment was evident in his voice.

Angling her head to one side, Daisy lifted a hand to the side of his face and reached up on tiptoe to kiss him on the corner of his mouth. "I'm not surprised. Truly. Which is the reason I wanted to do this with *you*, Alex."

"Still, you can't imagine us married, can you?" he asked, mostly as a test.

Daisy inhaled softly. "Can you?"

For a moment, Alex looked as if he had been given a test with no right answers. "We're not exactly the marrying type, are we?" he countered.

She shook her head. "At least, not yet," she murmured, glad to see the faintest hint that he was relieved. "Who knows, though?" Her fingers resumed their work on the fastenings of his breeches. She undid the top ones, but instead of moving to the other two, she gripped the fabric of his shirt and pulled it up in an effort to free it from its moorings. Before she could continue, Alex pulled the shirt from his body.

"Is it true I shouldn't kiss you?" she asked as her hands moved to press against his chest. Her fingers splayed and worked their way through the dark crisp curls that covered his chest. Her thumb slid over one of his nipples, and she heard as well as felt his slight inhalation of breath.

Perhaps seducing a man was easy. She considered what it might feel like to press her lips to the same nipple and flick her tongue over it. Would it taste of salt? Or something else? Something masculine, do doubt.

His spicy cologne, obviously applied with care since the entire room didn't smell like it, briefly wafted past her nose. She would have been lost to desire except Alex's voice brought her back to the here and now.

"KISSING IS… INTIMATE," he said. "More so than sexual intercourse," he added, hoping she wouldn't be bestowing kisses on the lips of the Marquess of Plymouth. A sensation he wasn't familiar with rose up in a sudden rush.

Envy.

Daisy would be doing *this* to the Marquess of Plymouth. Probably within a fortnight.

"Can I kiss you here?" she asked, placing her lips on his chest, very near one of his nipples.

"You can kiss me anywhere," he replied, hoping she understood his meaning. One of her fingers traced the silhouette of his arousal, and he hissed. "Including there," he added as his gaze went to the ceiling. If she continued what she was doing, he wouldn't make it to the bed.

"Or here?" Her lips clamped down on his other nipple, and he hissed.

"Anywhere," he whispered. Before he could allow her to do whatever she planned to do next, he moved to sit on the edge of the bed. He divested himself of his boots and stockings, his arousal making it difficult to bend over.

Daisy stood before him, reaching out to undo the last two buttons at the top of his breeches. "Will you tell me if I'm doing anything wrong?" she asked again.

A groan erupted from his throat. "I will," he replied before he stood and pulled the bed linens down from the pile of pillows at the head of the bed. "But you won't." When he turned back to her, he pushed the translucent dressing gown from her shoulders, heartened when she didn't fend off his move with half-hearted words or feeble attempts to stop him.

He was rather startled when her fingers hooked the top of his breeches and smalls and pushed them down over his muscled bottom and past his thick thighs. The sensation of her fingertips on his bare skin had him inhaling sharply.

Perhaps it had been too long since he'd last been with a woman. Perhaps he needed her more than he had thought. For overwhelming desire had him doing something he had never done with a woman before.

He took her mouth with his.

He kissed her, forcing his tongue between her startled lips. He tasted the champagne they had drunk. Sensed her surprise in her reaction. Held her close lest she attempt to push him away. And he was heartened when she responded to his kiss, her chest lifting to press against his, her hands wrapping around his shoulders in an attempt to hold on.

He wasn't about to allow her to escape.

He wasn't about to allow her to prevent him from removing the satin gown from her body before he moved her onto the bed.

Following her down, he growled when she spread her legs slightly, giving his the room they needed so he might do his worst. For a moment, he feared she might keep her eyes closed, or worse, stare at the ceiling, but her gaze stayed entirely on him.

He moved one of his hands to the space at the top of her thighs, and he reveled in the wetness he felt there. Reveled in how her chest lifted at his slight touch. Reveled in the inhalation of breath that sounded from her. Reveled when her legs spread wider and her knees bent.

Lightly brushing his fingers over her womanhood, he thrilled at feeling the swollen nubbin. He couldn't help the sense of triumph he felt when, after his middle finger had circled it slowly and rubbed over it, she gasped and the word, "Yes," hissed from her lips.

His head dropped, his lips claiming one of her nipples. He did with his tongue what she had done to his nipple, flicking over the engorged pebble until she mewled with need. His mouth moved to her other nipple, attempting to claim the entire breast as he supped and suckled. When she bucked beneath him, her mons pressing into his arousal, he knew he wouldn't last long.

Alex plunged his hardened manhood into her then, closing his eyes and holding his breath when it felt a slight resistance. Pulling out, he thrust into her again, this time seating his manhood fully into her warm, wet haven.

There wasn't anywhere else he wanted to be just then. Anywhere else in the world.

"Daisy," he said on a sigh as he stilled himself and took a moment to revel in the heat of her body. He began the rhythm he knew would bring him—and hopefully her—to ecstasy. A few thrusts, and he knew he would be spent. Knew he would come in a shower of bright lights and overwhelming sensations of pleasure that would extend from his core throughout his entire body.

But this was unlike anything he had ever experienced.

Tightness gripped him, prevented him from leaving her body. Ecstasy washed over him and through him, the light behind his closed eyes blinding before it was replaced with a thousand stars.

Unable to do more than collapse atop her, Alex groaned and lowered himself onto her soft body.

DAISY WATCHED as Alex's body ceased, suspended above her on what appeared to be a flash of pain. The cords of his neck were apparent, as was the strained expression on his face. She couldn't imagine this would be his ecstasy, but she remembered what her father had looked like when he was in the throes of passion with her mother. How he, too, would cease his movements, arch his back, and look as if he might die at any moment. Then his entire body would relax all at once, and he would collapse onto Lily Albright, his breathing labored and his body sweat-soaked.

He never stayed like that for long. He would stir and kiss her mother thoroughly. Murmur soft words of love and devotion, and eventually pull himself from her body. Then he would collapse onto the mattress next to her and allow an audible sigh of satisfaction before falling to sleep.

. . .

When Alex stirred, Daisy gripped him harder, hoping he wouldn't move from atop her. She was still growing used to having a foreign body inside her. Still questioning the sense of fullness she experienced. Wondering at the warmth that had flooded her insides the very moment of his ecstasy. Curious about the slight movements she felt as his manhood softened and the fullness subsided into a more comfortable sensation.

"You have to let go, my sweet, or I will end up sleeping atop you for the rest of the night," he whispered in warning.

Daisy moved a hand to to the back of his head, spearing his dark hair with her fingertips. "You say that as if it's a bad thing," she whispered.

She felt him chuckle, his entire body vibrating. "Minx," he murmured. When he did lift his head, he asked, "Am I allowed to stay?"

Daisy grinned at hearing his rebuke and his query as she lowered her knees down the side of his body until her feet touched the bed. "You had better."

"Oh, good, because I think I'm going to want you at least twice more before the sun comes up."

Daisy chuckled softly. Although she had been prepared for him, she had still felt the sharp pinch when his manhood penetrated her barrier on his second thrust. Felt the sudden fullness as he buried himself to the hilt inside her. Felt as if they had become one.

She couldn't imagine why he thought kissing was too intimate.

Oh, but the power she had felt upon clenching on his manhood! The knowledge that he had surrendered himself to her hold, collapsing atop her soft body. Giving himself body and soul to her hold.

She may not have felt the same pleasure he had imparted when he stroked her womanhood and then pressed on it with his finger, but at the moment, she didn't care. She no longer had to worry about her damned virginity. Concern herself with what her next assignments might have in store for her.

She had given her virtue to Alexander Bradley, and he hadn't seemed to have noticed.

CHAPTER 8
REVELATIONS AT MIDNIGHT

A couple of hours later

Soft snoring brought Daisy out of a light slumber. At some point the hour before, Alex had lowered himself to the bed at her side, wrapped an arm cross her waist, and cupped a breast with his hand. She didn't mind, except she wanted desperately to wash her nether region, especially since she was sure he would do something entirely different with her when he awoke.

Despite his possessive hold, Daisy managed to slip off the bed and make her way into the bathing chamber by the dim light from a single candle lamp. The tub still contained the bathwater in which she had bathed earlier that evening. She stepped into it, hissing as the cool water covered her lower legs. She welcomed the cold when she lowered her bottom into the water, though.

Although she hadn't felt pain upon her deflowering, she now experienced a sort of delicious soreness.

Her entire body buzzed, her skin tingled, and for a moment, she thought she was foxed. Since it had been hours since she had drunk the champagne, she decided the new awareness she experienced had to be from what Alex had done to her.

The reminder set off a most delightful frisson beneath her skin, and she inhaled softly. Would it always be like this? Think of that moment when he had touched her most private place and experience a dart of pure pleasure?

She leaned back in the tub and was about to imagine it again when footfalls had her on alert. A moment later, and Alex appeared as a silhouette on the threshold.

He did not look happy.

ALEX KNEW the moment Daisy had slipped from his hold. The warmth beneath his arm and at the front of his body dissipated, and he sighed with disappointment. When he heard the muted splashing of water in the bathing chamber, he understood why she had left the bed.

The thought of what he would do next with her had his cock rising in anticipation. Deciding he would help her from the tub—assist with drying her off by offering her a linen—he pushed the bed linens off his body. He was about to make his way to her when his attention went to the bed. To the small dark stain that marred the expanse of white linen.

A rock seemed to drop in his stomach at the same moment a flash of annoyance had him seething.

He stepped into the bathing chamber, intending to scold Daisy. For a moment, he thought she had trapped him. Talked him into bedding her so that he would offer for her hand.

But they had discussed marriage. Come to the same conclusion. Neither one of them were marriage material. So... why had she come to him?

"What's wrong?" Daisy asked as she straightened in the tub. She didn't try to hide her nakedness, but then it was nearly dark in the bathing chamber. She hadn't lit another candle lamp.

"I took your virtue," he hissed.

Daisy audibly sighed before carefully standing up. "I *gave* you my virtue," she countered, trying not to sound impatient. She reached for a bath linen. "You cannot take what is freely given," she added as she quickly dried her legs and bottom. Then she wrapped the linen around her middle and moved to stand before him.

For once, she wished she was at least six inches taller.

"You should have told me, Daisy," he argued, struggling to keep his voice down.

"And if I had? Would you have come here tonight?"

Alex looked as if she had slapped him across the face. "I... I cannot say for sure," he stammered.

"If not you, Alex, I would have had to find someone else," she whispered hoarsely. "I could not go on this mission as a virgin."

"You could have turned down the mission," he countered. He knew immediately how his comment sounded and rolled his eyes. Daisy would never turn down an assignment, nor would he. "I apologize," he said on a sigh.

"Please, don't be angry with me," she whispered.

The fight seemed to go out of him all at once as Daisy wrapped her arms around his chest and pressed her linen-clad body to his. "I've a mind to... to punish you for this," he murmured.

Frissons darted beneath her skin, and Daisy looked up in alarm. "What... what do you have in mind?" She didn't mean to sound excited, but his hardened manhood, pressing into her belly as it was, had her curious.

"Oh, no," he whispered. "I'm not going to tell you."

Daisy let out a squeak when he lifted her into his arms and took her to the bed. He dumped her onto it, pulling the linen away from her body. Her hair, no longer caught up in a bun, spread over the linens in a dark halo around her head, and her arms were splayed out on either side of her body. He lifted her knees, moving them so they were bent over his shoulders while he watched her hands grip the linens, as if she knew she had to anchor herself to the bed for what was to come.

"Hold on," he warned before his head disappeared between her thighs.

His tongue on her womanhood had Daisy crying out, her chest rising from the bed even as his hands kept her hips pinned down. Knowing he had pressed too hard to start, he softened his touch, merely circled the spot a few times with the tip of his tongue before he pushed it into her yet again. She cried out and then mewled softly as her ambrosia coated his tongue. He knew the moment she was on the verge of her orgasm. Knew because he felt her inner muscles attempt to pull him in farther.

He denied her the pleasure, though, and instead covered her womanhood with his lips to suckle her softly. Flicked his tongue over it once, twice. He was about to again but he knew *he* couldn't hold on much longer. She was already lost to an ecstasy he could only hope to sustain with what he was about to do to her.

Flipping her over onto her stomach, Alex used one arm to lift her hips from the bed. He pulled her closer to the edge and drove his manhood into her in one hard, unforgiving thrust.

He watched as she once again gripped the bed linens, and he paused to slide the palm of one hand down her back along the bumps of her spine. Knowing she couldn't see what he was doing, he slid the same hand around the side of her body and beneath one breast. His fingers splayed until he had a nipple trapped between two, and he gently squeezed them together.

The sound of her whimper had him pulling his hand away. When one of her hands gave up its hold on the bed and moved to cup his balls, it was nearly his undoing. At the sound of his growl, she let go. "Minx," he ground out.

Not about to give in to his release as easily as he had before—he wanted her to experience what he was about to—Alex finally pulled out and thrust into her again and again, listening to her shallow breathing and her cries of 'yes' and her soft begging for more. He touched her where their bodies met, and he set off her ecstasy before he finally took his own.

CHAPTER 9
THE WEE SMALL HOURS OF
THE MORNING

Just before dawn the following day

As he had promised the night before, Alex made love to Daisy one more time before he took his leave of her and of the Soho Club. This time, his moves had been slow and quiet, his words tender and his touch even more so.

When they lay together in the aftermath, Daisy half covering his body and their legs intertwined, Alex swallowed and said, "I've been an ass."

Daisy lifted her head from the small of his shoulder. "What are you talking about?"

He turned to stare at her. "You must be terribly sore. I didn't even think about..." His words were cut off when she placed a finger over his lips.

"I'm fine, Alex."

"I've never bedded a virgin before."

Blinking at hearing his claim, Daisy settled her head back onto his chest. "Did you wish to save yourself for a wife then?" she asked, making sure it didn't sound like a tease.

He gave her a quelling glance. "I guess I would have expected a virgin to be less... *willing*," he stammered. "Less seductive."

"Hmm," she sighed. "Will you come back tonight?"

For the longest time, Alex was quiet. When he finally spoke, he said, "If I don't, are you going to invite someone else to join you in this bed?"

Daisy tittered. "No, of course not."

"That's my new fear for you now, you must know," he whispered.

"What do you mean?"

"Now that you're not a virgin, you'll go off and become a celebrated courtesan, or... or make your living as a mistress. You could certainly make more than you do working for Home."

The words struck a bit too close, not only given her next assignment, but also what her mother had been before she'd found a protector that kept her out of the business for the rest of her life. Lily Albright had been a courtesan because her mother had been one in the French court.

If her father had been anyone other than who he was, Daisy would have been a courtesan or a mistress, sold off to some middle-aged minor aristocrat.

"Until last night, you didn't think I was a virgin," she

reminded him. "In fact, why did you think I was already ruined?"

Alex inhaled softly. "The business we're in, I suppose. Your age. You've been on the Continent. It's a wonder you made it back to British shores without being tupped by some frog," he murmured.

Daisy made a sound of disgust. "I would have killed him before he could get my skirts up," she claimed.

Giving a start beneath her, Alex tightened his hold on her. "Have you killed a man?"

She shook her head. "I shot a man once, but if he died, it happened much later."

"You weren't a guttersnipe, were you?"

Lifting her head once again, Daisy stared at Alex. "Whatever gave you that idea?"

Alex shrugged in the bed before rising up onto an elbow, which sent Daisy rolling onto her back. "You were an orphan, though?" he half-asked.

She inhaled to respond, deciding she could admit some of her secrets. "My mother died when I was young, but my father raised my sister and me."

"You have a sister?"

"Diana, yes," she replied. "She's a teacher of arithmetic and dancing."

"You're joking," he whispered.

"I am not," she replied, suppressing a yawn.

"Where does she live?"

"Here in London." The reminder that she was back in the capital had Daisy thinking she should pay a call on Diana before she left for Yorkshire. If she was vague enough with the details, she wouldn't have to be concerned about her mission vexing her father. "She knows I work for Home, but... I think she believes I work as a secretary."

"Better she not know the truth," he warned.

"Well, I certainly won't be the one to tell her."

"What about your father?"

Daisy stiffened. "What about him?"

"Is *he* still alive?"

She inhaled softly. "Come back tonight, and I'll tell you tomorrow morning," she replied.

Alex's eyes darted to where the bed linens barely covered her breasts. When they narrowed, he said, "I could force the information from you." He pushed the bed linens down and covered a nipple with his mouth, which had Daisy giggling softly.

"Will you come?" she asked when he finally gave up his hold on her and settled back onto the bed.

"In more ways than one," he replied before he finally removed himself from the bed.

When he was mostly dressed, Daisy retrieved the cravat from where she had left it draped over a chair and joined him. Standing before him, she carefully pleated it before standing on tiptoe to wrap it around his neck. She wound each end around twice before tying it into a perfect mail coach knot. Then she buttoned his waistcoat.

She stepped back to admire her work, well aware

Alex was once again aroused. "What is it?" she asked when he simply stared at her. She glanced down, realizing she was still naked.

"You make an excellent valet, my lady, but I fear I would never leave for work if I hired you." He kissed her forehead before retrieving his cane and top hat.

"What about the satchel?" Daisy asked before he reached the door.

"Oh, the paperwork, you mean? That's your assignment for the day," he replied before he bowed and left the room.

Daisy's eyes widened when she opened the leather bag.

Assignment for the day?

She was sure it would take far longer to complete.

CHAPTER 10

THE JOB ISN'T DONE UNTIL
THE PAPERWORK IS

A half hour later

*D*ressed in a serviceable gown with her hair done up in a bun atop her head, Daisy opened the satchel and hissed at the sight of the papers, ink, and a pen therein.

Mr. Bradley hadn't been teasing when he had warned her she would have to do his paperwork. Despite the night they had spent together—and what she had given up to him—Daisy found she couldn't think of him as 'Alex' by the light of day.

Settling the contents of the satchel onto the dressing table, she was about to read the top paper when a knock sounded at the door.

Thinking perhaps Mr. Bradley had returned, she called out, "Come."

"Pardon, miss, but Mrs. Skarsgard wanted me to

remind you 'bout breakfast." The young woman, garbed in a drab gown and white apron, reminded Daisy of a street urchin she had once known. "Cook will make you whatever ye'd like. Cup of chocolate, too."

The mention of chocolate had Daisy's stomach rumbling. Out of nervousness, she hadn't eaten any dinner the night before, and her nocturnal activities with Alex had only increased her appetite. "How are the kitchens here?" Daisy asked.

"Oh, very good, miss. Seein' as how we have staff and our other overnight guests, our cook is a good 'un. I can service your room whilst you eat, if you'd like."

Daisy thought of the water in the tub and the mussed linens on the bed. Although she had done a serviceable job putting them to rights, fresh bed linens would be welcome. "Very well," she said. She stuffed the papers back into the satchel, not about to leave them while she vacated the room. "Could you tell me where breakfast is served?"

"The dining room is just downstairs, miss. Bottom of the stairs to the right."

"Will I need any money to pay for it?" Daisy asked, thinking to take her reticule. She had stashed the reticule in the bottom of her valise, a small pocket knife set so someone rifling through the luggage would be stabbed before they reached her money.

"Oh, no, miss. Your meals are included as part of your stay, of course," the maid replied, already seeing to unmaking the bed. There was no indication she noticed the bloodstain.

"Thank you," Daisy said before she lifted the handle of the satchel to her shoulder. Her thoughts went to how much the accommodations might have cost the Home Office. How much they must have trusted Mrs. Skarsgard and her retinue of employees to house an operative for a few day's time.

Certainly they wouldn't have known of her personal mission, though. The one she was engaged in with Mr. Bradley.

She made her way down the hall, calling out a "Good morning" to Mrs. Skarsgard when she caught sight of the woman through the open door of her office.

"Good morning," Mrs. Skarsgard replied, her response muted now that Daisy had begun descending the stairs. The scent of fresh baking bread had Daisy inhaling deeply.

At the bottom of the carpeted staircase, Daisy looked to the right and paused. The small dining room was far more elegant than one meant for merely staff and a few guests. Thick velvet drapes were pulled back from white Austrian sheers covering the three windows. The filtered sunshine bathed the room in a soft light.

Three other guests were sitting at one table, their heads bent together in conversation not meant to be overheard. Honoring their wish, Daisy moved to the farthest table from them and was about to take a seat when a footman seemed to appear from nowhere. He pulled the chair from the table for her. "Good morning, my lady. What can I bring you for breakfast?"

Remembering the maid's comment that they would make anything, Daisy said, "A cup of chocolate, a boiled egg, toast, grilled tomato, and..." She glanced up at him. "Ham?"

"Very good, my lady," he replied, before giving a bow and then hurrying off.

Daisy had to resist the urge to giggle.

A proper breakfast. She hadn't had one in an age.

She pulled a couple of sheets from the satchel and began to read. She wasn't done with the third sheet when a steaming cup of chocolate was set before her. Another page, and the entire breakfast—far more food than she had seen in a week—appeared.

"Oh!" she said when she saw the size of the toast. The slice of ham. The tomato. Even the egg seemed larger than normal.

"Should you require more, you only need ring," the footman said as he placed a bell on the white linen tablecloth.

Torn between turning her entire attention to the meal and continuing her reading, Daisy realized she would have to do both in order to make it through all the papers that Mr. Bradley had left her.

By the fifth page, just as she was finishing a slice of toast, Daisy wondered if the operative knew exactly what he had given her. The first few pages were merely briefs —updates on ongoing investigations being done by operatives of the Foreign Office. Good to know, but not necessarily of use to her.

The fifth page was actually Mr. Bradley's orders for the upcoming mission. Her eyes rounded at reading the details—take on the persona of Captain Jack Crawley, take command of the former naval ship, now christened *Molly*, and patrol the shores off Yorkshire in pursuit of smugglers.

The next sheet detailed what had been surmised about their prey. Smugglers from France, running liquor across the Channel, then up to Yorkshire, and depositing it on shore somewhere along a stretch of coastline that was as long as twenty miles. The most likely landing point was on a beach in an inlet that provided some coverage.

A beach which fell within the Marquess of Plymouth's lands.

Daisy was quick to think that the beach might be remote enough from Plymouth's home at Castle Keyes to be unknown to the marquess.

But once it reached land, how was the liquor being transported all the way to Scarborough?

She studied a map, conveniently stuffed in between the next pages of the brief. When she lifted the next sheet from the stack, her eyes rounded at seeing a portrait drawing of Ethan Range, Marquess of Plymouth. The artist's rendering was obviously done for the purpose of painting the man's portrait.

A hand went to her middle. How could a mere image

of the marquess have frissons shooting through her core? She supposed her reaction to him was much like the one she experienced with Alex—at that moment, she couldn't think of him as Mr. Bradley—and yet the two only shared a hair style in common. She studied his features. Plymouth's jaw was squarer, his eyes wider set. He was handsome, but not in the usual aristocratic way. In fact, he didn't look anything like the aristocrats in London. No hooked nose. Darker hair, given how his short-cropped waves were drawn—not blonde. A body that might have been guilty of hard labor, or at least of riding a horse every day. Given the size of his marquessate, it wasn't unexpected.

She quickly read the details of the Plymouth marquessate. Coal mines were the primary source of income—and problems. Between mine collapses, a recent fire, and shortages of labor, it was a wonder they provided any income at all.

Was this why Home suspected he was running illegal liquor? To cover the losses from the coal mines?

The marquess had never been suspected of illegal activities in the past. His father had been a bit of a reprobate, though, gambling until most of the unentailed properties were divested by way of card games and bets on horse races.

The dowager marchioness, his mother, was apparently ensconced in a well-appointed cottage located on the outskirts of the marquessate, but close enough to a town to provide entertainments and...

Daisy blinked.

"A string of lovers?" she whispered in shock.

"Would you like more chocolate?" the footman asked quietly. "Or breakfast? Perhaps some shortbread?"

Blinking, Daisy stared into her empty cup, wondering how she could have drained it without realizing it. Then her gaze went to her plate. She had eaten almost everything on it. "More chocolate would be divine," she murmured. "I suppose I should have some shortbread, and coffee, if it's available."

"Of course, my lady."

The footman hurried off, and Daisy noted the three people who had been there when she had arrived were no longer in the room.

She was the only one there.

How had she missed their departure? She was usually far more aware of her surroundings. Far more attuned to what was happening around her.

Her attention returned to the briefs. The next few pages were letters which required responses. She set them aside, deciding she could pen something that would be appropriate and have Mr. Bradley sign them when he returned to the club that night.

The next page had her tittering just as the footman returned with the cups of coffee and chocolate and the plate of shortbread. "Pray tell, how is it your cook knows how to make shortbread?" she asked. She had thought it only available in Scotland.

"I rather doubt I can wrest the secret from him, my lady," the footman replied in an apologetic tone.

Daisy arched a dark brow and shoo'd him away, returning her attention to the paper that had her amused when the footman appeared.

If you've made it this far, you're to be commended. Show me this page, and I shall reward you. — Alex

A frisson passed through her middle at the thought of what her reward might be.

A repeat of what he had done to her after she bathed? Something he hadn't yet done to her?

Daisy was about to imagine far more when her attention went to the next sheet, and her mind focussed on the matter at hand.

Service to King and Country.

She read a copy of a letter that had been sent to Viscount Chamberlain from his counterpart at the Home Office, requesting help on this mission. One particular paragraph caught her attention.

Given the marquess is not married and not currently engaging in any affaires, at least none known to Mr. Snelling, it is our opinion a female be employed to act in the capacity of a mistress. We have an agent in mind for said position. Since she was previously employed by your office, should you know of a reason Miss Albright not be consid-

ered in this capacity, your response is required as soon as possible.

Daisy inhaled and immediately wondered if Chamberlain had replied. She had always suspected the viscount knew who her father was. If he had read the letter, she was sure he would have warned the Home Office of possible repercussions.

Since she had been given the assignment, perhaps Lord Chamberlain didn't know. Or perhaps his response hadn't reached Home in time. Or...

Mayhap she was simply the best female for the job, regardless of her father's identity.

She had promised Mr. Bradley she would tell him her father's name tomorrow morning. Now she wished she had promised it for the morning she was to board the mail coach to Scarborough. Ensure she had another night with him.

Another frisson passed through her body. She could hardly wait for his arrival that evening.

Determined to prove her skills at seduction, she had already decided she would wear the sheer wrapper that came with the white gown, but not the white gown beneath it. Greet him at the door with a glass of the brandy she had discovered amongst the liquor decanters on the sideboard.

She tried to imagine how he might respond. Would he scold her? Kiss her? Drain the brandy, take her into his arms and toss her onto the bed?

In middle of eating the shortbread, Daisy found she was spending far too much time thinking of Alex.

She should be considering the matter at hand. The mission. Who might have been assigned if she wasn't.

Who else fit the profile?

She knew a few of the other female agents who worked for both the Home and Foreign Offices, not that there were many. One was far too old to play the role of a mistress. Another was already on an assignment on the Continent. Yet another had just given birth to her third child and was tucked away in a cottage in Wiltshire with her doting husband, a baron who probably had no idea what she had done for the Foreign Office in her younger years.

Then there was Lydia Barrymore. Daisy had no idea where the newly widowed viscountess was at the moment, but Lady Barrymore would have been the only other operative she knew of that might qualify for such an assignment.

The orders had come to Daisy, though.

Noting she had finished eating everything that had been placed before her, Daisy stuffed the papers into the satchel and made her way back to her room.

The maid had already completed her duties, the room restored to the way it had appeared when Daisy had arrived the day before.

Spreading the pages out on various pieces of furniture, Daisy concentrated on writing letters and reviewing the remaining pages in the satchel. She was about to consider going to the dining room for some supper when a knock sounded at the door.

Thinking it was the maid sent to remind her about dinner, she was stunned when she found Alexander Bradley leaning against the door jamb. She wondered if he was stopping on his way to an evening entertainment until she took a quick look at the clock on the mantel.

She gasped.

How could it already be nine o'clock?

CHAPTER 11
ONE LAST NIGHT TOGETHER

A moment later

"Oh, forgive me, I've lost track of time," Daisy said as she opened the door wider.

"Do tell," Alex replied, his brows furrowing in obvious disappointment.

Daisy glanced down at her day gown and hissed. "Would you be amenable to... to going to the dining room? For ten minutes? They have shortbread," she said, as if it was the best food in the world. "It would give me enough time to change clothes."

His gaze went to the array of papers spread throughout the room. "Oh," he murmured. "You haven't had dinner, have you?" he guessed.

"I haven't, but I had the most amazing breakfast," she replied.

"Daisy…" he said on a sigh.

"Here. Take these with you," she said as she gathered the letters she had written and paired them with the ones that needed responses. "These require your signature."

"I'm not going anywhere," he said as he closed the door and removed his greatcoat.

Daisy's eyes rounded at seeing the formal clothes he wore. "Did you come from a ball?"

He allowed a smirk as he stepped up and kissed her on the forehead.

"What was that for?" she asked.

"With any luck, you'll receive such a greeting from your employer up north," Alex replied. "I just came from my club. I had the good fortune to pester a certain viscount regarding his behavior with his long-time mistress."

"Behavior?" Daisy repeated, a brow furrowing.

"Every man who employs a mistress has different expectations of her," he replied. "All spelled out in a written contract. Turns out, for some, it's just a bi-weekly tryst. They have no contact with one another outside of what they do in her townhouse on those occasions."

Daisy listened patiently, deciding it was better he not know that she was very familiar with the life of a courtesan. Her mother had been sure to tell Daisy and her sister about the lifestyle that could be both rewarding and dangerous, heartbreaking and lonely. "And for others?" she prompted.

"Some men love their mistresses. Live with them. Have children with them. The only reason they don't marry them is because... well, they're already married," he stammered.

Sometimes they weren't.

Daisy's father certainly hadn't been. And he and her mother might have eventually wed if her father wasn't who he was. He wouldn't have been allowed to marry a courtesan, though. Not given the title he would inherit. Had since inherited. "Or they cannot, because Society would not allow it," she said.

Alex regarded her with a long look before he nodded. "Spoken as if you're familiar with that particular situation."

Daisy remembered her promise to him—that she would tell him who her father was the next morning. "I am." She glanced over at the array of papers laid out on every available horizontal surface. "But that's not what's important right now. Have you read any of this?" she asked.

Sighing, Alex pointed to several papers. "My orders, the brief about Plymouth, and the letters. Thank you for penning the responses, by the way."

"You're welcome," she said. "I left the most important sheets on top. I'll be ready in ten minutes." She turned to go into the bathing chamber, but Alex hooked one of her arms with his.

"This..." He paused as he waved to the paperwork. "This isn't exactly titillating," he complained.

"No, but I will be," she countered before she shook off his hold. "Oh, and I found your note. I can hardly wait to discover what you have in store for me this evening." She waggled her eyebrows before she disappeared into the bathing chamber.

Alex gave her a look of appreciation, the first sign of it since his arrival. Deciding he best see to what he could whilst she was changing—he imagined her wearing a white gown since she had mentioned purchasing one—Alex turned his attention to the letters he needed to sign. Chuckling as he wrote his signature—all of them were appropriately written and as vague as they needed to be —he turned his attention to the papers he hadn't so much as looked at the afternoon before.

He was actually reading one in its entirety when Daisy emerged from the bathing chamber.

Her hair was no longer pinned up, the dark mane ending well past her shoulders. Instead of wearing one of the gowns she had purchased, Daisy wore only the white gown's sheer wrapper. The front edges and neckline were trimmed in a soutache braid, as was the bottom hem, but otherwise there was nothing else to the garment. Her nakedness was apparent despite the room's dim lighting, especially when she made her way in his direction. The edges of the gown fluttered to the sides, leaving the front of her body entirely exposed.

A choking sound erupted from Alex's throat as Daisy stepped up to him and began undoing the knot at his neck. "Promise me you won't wear that the first time you're with him," he whispered.

The oddest sensation swept through Daisy just then. "I think I shall wait and see how it goes when I meet the marquess," she replied. "You're not going to be jealous?" she half-asked.

"Maybe." His fingers fumbled with his top coat buttons.

Daisy swallowed, surprised he didn't simply deny it. "Have you been looking forward to spending the evening with me?" A quick glance down, and she could see his manhood straining the black satin breeches.

Alex struggled with the waistcoat buttons. "You've no idea," he replied in a hoarse whisper.

Unwinding the black silk cravat from around his neck, Daisy paused and angled her head to one side. For a moment, she felt guilty. She hadn't given him much in the way of any thought since that morning, her attentions entirely on the papers.

Now that he was standing before her, the scent of his cologne surrounding her, she felt her body react. Felt her nipples tighten and her insides turn molten. The skin on her lower arms turned to gooseflesh. The space at the top of her thighs began to throb.

Would it always be like this with him? With any other man? She had never experienced sensations like those that coursed beneath her skin.

Working faster, she had the cravat removed and was

pulling on the tails of his shirt when he stilled her hands with his own. "Promise me, Daisy," he whispered.

She furrowed her dark brows and finally nodded. "I promise, I won't wear it. Unless I'm wearing the nightrail beneath it," she clarified.

He let go of her hands. "I've been thinking—"

"Oh, dear," she murmured.

He moved to the edge of the bed and shed his shoes and stockings. "Given the business we're in, neither one of us will likely marry."

"True," Daisy replied, reaching out to do undo the fastenings at the top of his breeches.

"You'll no doubt gain another assignment right after this one," he went on. He pushed down the breeches, freeing his manhood. Daisy saw to removing the clothes completely and then draped them on the back of a chair before turning to take him in hand.

"As will you."

"I think I have at least five more years in me." He jerked as her hold on his manhood tightened.

"Oh, I would have thought ten or twenty," Daisy countered, her attention on his member. On how the skin was stretched taut over what felt like bone but couldn't be. On how the simplest of touches had it reacting, especially those along the back of it and at its very tip. How it had him hissing and groaning.

"Field work, I meant," he whispered, struggling to breathe.

Daisy paused in her ministrations and finally gave

him her full attention. She gave a start when he dropped his forehead to hers. "Five years," she agreed.

"Don't think me daft, but... I think we would suit one another."

Staring at him, Daisy slowly furrowed her brows. "Are you... proposing marriage?" She said it with a hint of annoyance, enough so he was forced to shake his head.

"A... a pact, merely."

"Go on."

He inhaled when she squeezed his manhood, and something that sounded like a cross between a blessing and a curse sounded from his lips. "If neither one of us has married someone else within the next five years, then we shall seek out one another and determine then if we still suit," he proposed. "Then decide if we... should marry."

Daisy considered his proposition a moment. It couldn't hurt to agree. They would certainly enjoy one another's company in a bedchamber. Their shared experiences as agents would mean they wouldn't have to keep secrets from one another.

Then Daisy remembered what she still had to tell him in the morning. "May I think on it?" she asked. She lowered her lips to the tip of his cock and kissed it.

Alex managed a strangled, affirmative sound.

"Now, what does it mean to 'ride St. George'? In bed, I mean," she asked, hoping to put his mind back on the matter at hand.

Chuckling, Alex lay back on the bed and pulled her atop him. "Straddle me, my fearless fairy, and ride me like the noble steed I am," he teased. He let out an *oomph* when she impaled herself on his manhood, and all thoughts of their mission left his head.

CHAPTER 12
CONFESSIONS OF A DAUGHTER

Dawn, the following morning

As gray light appeared framed in the room's only window, Alex stirred. So did his cock.

"I was beginning to wonder if you were ever going to wake up," Daisy whispered.

"What is it? What's wrong?" he asked, rising onto one elbow.

"I need you," she whispered, one of her hands sliding down his sleep-warm skin to his erection.

"Again?" he asked, his face lighting up at hearing her plea.

"I cannot help it. You smell divine, and you've spoiled me rotten with whatever you did to me last night."

Alex chuckled at the thought of what he had done after she had ridden him to completion.

He had tupped her over the edge of the bed, not an

easy feat given her short stature. Used his hand to pleasure her until she begged him to stop and then made love to her as fast and as furiously as he could, his need had been so great.

Now when she spread her legs beneath him, he decided he only had strength enough for slow and quiet.

He adored her quiet mewls. The sounds of her slight inhalations. The way she begged and then thanked him after he had seen to her pleasure.

No other lover had ever thanked him before.

She would no doubt curse him when he told her he had to leave for Wapping later that morning. New orders had arrived, and the *Molly* was due to leave dock when the tide went out.

He still had to apply his gold caps over his front teeth, pack a bag with his Jack Crawley garb, and inform Arthur's he would be away for a time.

Thrusting into her several more times, he thrilled at feeling how her back arched beneath him as his thumb caressed the place where their bodies met. Thrilled at hearing her keening and crying as his touch set off her orgasm.

His own release had spasms of pleasure seizing his movements for what he hoped might be eternity. Stars filled his field of vision. The world stopped. Quiet surrounded him.

Reality resumed, however, and he lowered himself atop her on a sigh of frustration.

Although he desperately wanted to sleep, there was much to do on this day.

"Please stay in me for just a while longer," Daisy whispered.

"I would be a fool to turn down such a request," he murmured. He propped his chest up on his elbows and stared down at her. She didn't look like what he had always imagined a mistress would look like, but she certainly acted in a manner that would suit the matter at hand. "Especially when..." He let the words trail off until she prompted him to continue. "I have new orders. Updated orders, rather."

Daisy stiffened beneath him. "When do you have to leave?"

"This afternoon. When the tide goes out," he replied.

She nodded in the pillow. "I go tomorrow on the mail coach," she said. "I'll be traveling for four days, I think."

"Is there anyone you must tell about your impending departure?"

Her eyes widened before she let out a loud sigh. "My father, I suppose. Although he cannot know that I'm to be Plymouth's mistress," she whispered.

"Why is that?"

He felt her jerk, and he was about to pull himself from her, but her hands gripped his buttocks. "Stay, please."

"All right," he whispered. "You said you would tell me who he is," he reminded her.

"Ariley," Daisy said, without preamble.

His brows furrowing, Alex stared down at her before a grin split his face. "For a moment there, I thought you were saying your father is the Duke of Ariley." He continued to grin until he saw her nod in the pillows. Quickly sobering, he was about to launch himself off the bed, but Daisy tightened her hold on him.

"My mother was Lily Albright. A courtesan. He was in love with her. She gave him two daughters, and then she died, and he continued to live with us until his father died, and then he had to come to London, but by then we were old enough to—"

"I'm as good as dead, aren't I?" Alex asked in dismay.

"No," she replied with a scoff. "He doesn't know about this. And I'm not about to tell him what I'm to do in Yorkshire."

Alex's attention had gone to a memory, though. To the moment he had mentioned to Lord Chamberlain that Daisy would be going to Scarborough. That flicker of shock and then what appeared to be relief on his face before he headed back to his office. "He knows you're going, though."

Daisy gasped. "But not—"

"No," Alex said with a quick shake of his head. "He just thinks you're being assigned to Snelling's office."

"Are you talking about my father? Or Lord Chamberlain?"

He gave her a quelling glance. Surely Chamberlain would be informing the duke that his daughter was going on another mission. "Both."

"Well, it's a relief if all they know about is Snelling."

"You father knows you're an operative?"

Nodding, Daisy said, "It doesn't matter that he's a duke—"

"It matters," Alex countered. "My god, Daisy."

"I was never going to be the English miss looking to marry and have babies," she countered. "He knows that. I'm a bastard. Even he would be hard pressed to find a fat, balding viscount willing to take me to wife."

"He would be a very lucky man," Alex whispered.

Daisy ignored the interruption. "I pleaded with Ariley several years ago to let me work for King and Country. Convinced him I would follow in my mother's footsteps if I wasn't allowed to have my way."

Alex stared at her for several seconds before he swallowed. "And here you are, following in her footsteps," he murmured. He wrapped his hands behind her back and rolled over onto his, bringing her body along so she was left on top of him.

"It's not like that," she argued as she speared his dark hair with her fingers and scraped his scalp with her nails. She grinned at hearing his hiss and feeling how his cock came alive again inside her. "But I understand if you've changed your mind about what we discussed last night."

A look of hurt crossed his face. "Oh, Daisy, I haven't changed my mind. I might suffer your father's wrath, though, should he ever learn about what we've done these past two nights."

Daisy shook her head. "We're in the Soho Club," she reminded him. "Our secrets are safe."

He finally nodded in the pillow. "Then before we leave each other's company for a time, will you do to me again what you did last night?"

One brow arching in delight, Daisy said, "You mean when you were St. George, my noble steed?"

He grinned. "That one, yes."

Daisy happily complied.

AFTER ALEX HAD DRESSED and gathered up his papers, he embraced Daisy and kissed her quite thoroughly. "I'll be watching for you from the water," he said as he pressed his forehead to hers.

"I'll look for your ship from the moors," she replied with a grin.

When Alex finally took his leave of her and of the Soho Club, Daisy inhaled deeply, as if to capture the scent of him one last time.

Although she had feared she would be sad to see him go, Daisy found she wasn't. They had left one another's company in good spirits, and they had a plan for a possible future together.

Five years wasn't so very long to wait, after all.

To LEARN what happens next for these two operatives, be sure to read *The Passion of a Marquess*, *The Epiphany of an Explorer*, and *The Conundrum of a Clerk*.

All three books are available from your favorite retailer.

ABOUT LINDA RAE SANDE

A self-described nerd and student of history, Linda Rae spent many years as a technical writer specializing in 3D graphics workstations, software and 3D animation (her movie credits include SHREK and SHREK 2). Getting lost in the rabbit holes of research has resulted in historical romances set in the Regency, Victorian, and Ancient Greece eras.

A fan of action-adventure movies, she can frequently be found at the local cinema. Although she no longer has any fish, she follows the San Jose Sharks. She is a member of Novelists, Inc. (NINC) and makes her home in Cody, Wyoming. More on her upcoming books can be found on her website: www.lindaraesande.com.

You can join her reader newsletter here: https://www.subscribepage.com/regency-romance-with-a-twist-newsletter-subscription

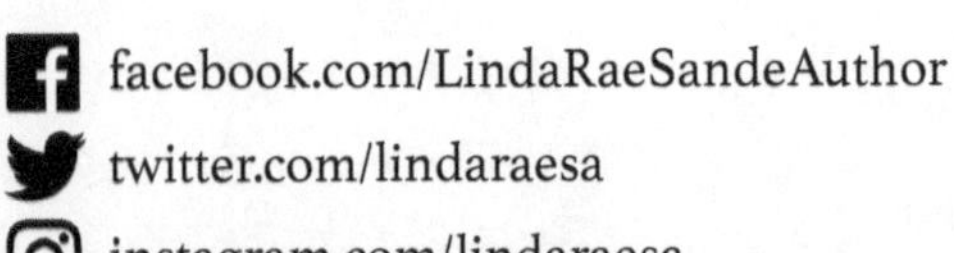

facebook.com/LindaRaeSandeAuthor

twitter.com/lindaraesa

instagram.com/lindaraesa